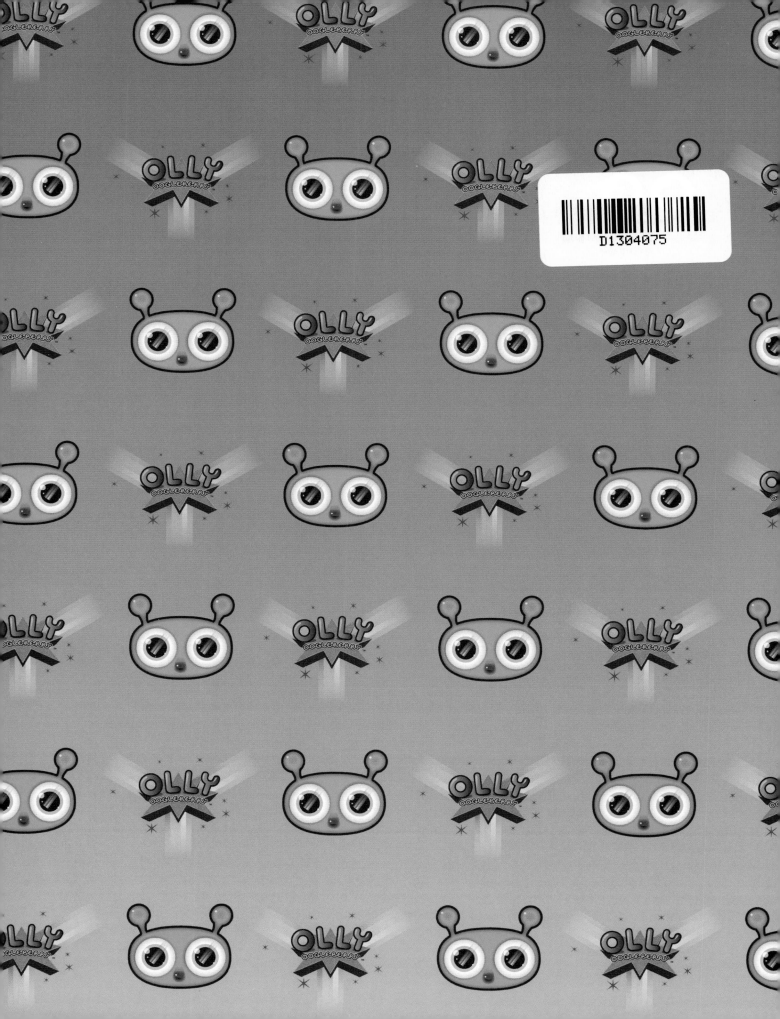

For my daughters, Vaden and Easley, who inspired me to rediscover a 30 year old dream and Kathryn, my incredibly supportive partner on this life's journey.

THE FABULOUS ADVENTURES OF
OLLY OOGLEBERRY:
MISSION TO SAVE EARTH

Conceived, Created and Written by Lou Hughes
Illustrated by Jonathan Ball
Layout Design by Saman Rooeintan

Second Edition
ISBN: 0615569536
EAN: 978-0615569536
LCCN: 2011943990
Library of Congress Cataloging-in-Publication Data on file.

Visit www.TickleMeSilly.Com and www.OllyOogleberry.Com

VISIT:
WWW.TICKLEMESILLY.COM
AND
WWW.OLLYOOGLEBERRY.COM

THE DAWDLING OF A RESTLESS SEVENTH GRADER. THAT WAS HOW IT ALL STARTED. 1981.

Olly Oogleberry was just one of thousands of childhood scribbles and random drawings. All of them long forgotten, except for this one timeless shape with an indescribably unique name that continued to fascinate me and percolate in my memory for the next 30 years.

I wasn't sure what Olly Oogleberry was when I first sketched his oval head, two antennae and big dreamy eyes at the ripe old age of 12. And never in my wildest dreams would I have ever imagined this curious and lovable alien amounting to anything — at least until my two children came into this world.

When my children were born I realized that the name and iconic shape that had captured my imagination for so many years was a reflection of a spirit inside me. And for that matter, the spirit inside every exhilarated, anxious, uncertain, and yet hopeful adolescent. I was a wanna-be adventurer longing to be anywhere else other than seventh grade math class. It was my imagination that took me where I wanted to go. And Olly came along for the ride.

Fast-forward to 2003 and the birth of our first daughter. As every parent knows, there's a sacred bedtime ritual. First, a bath, and then a few bedtime stories. My daughters and I began concocting our own bedtime tales featuring my curious and lovable childhood creation. Each night we would see who could tell the most enrapturing story full of earthly wonders and aliens from distant galaxies.

I created Olly Oogleberry as a vessel for learning about the extraordinary universe in which we live, and our tiny, yet meaningful place in it. Olly is an ambassador to help us open our eyes, when they are sometimes closed, to all that is good and wonderful in this world (and the great beyond). Regardless of our differences, whether they may be age, color, country, or our position in society, the human spirit remains the same. We all struggle with who we are, why we're here and the hope that our lives will be filled with wonder, joy and a sense of connection.

There's an Olly in every one of us yearning to find (or rediscover) our true selves — our inner dreamer and adventurer. Grab a hold of your dreams, hopes and aspirations and don't let go. Olly Oogleberry is evidence — that even after 30 long years — anyone can realize a lifelong dream. Olly and I both know that one day your wildest dreams will come true, too.

Lou Hughes,
Creator of Olly Oogleberry

LOCATED 11.2 MILLION LIGHT YEARS FROM EARTH, PLANET OOGLEBERRY IS A MAGICAL, MYSTICAL PLANET FORMED BY TRILLIONS OF PINK AND PURPLE TRANSLUCENT CRYSTALS, BEAUTIFUL RAINBOWS, FIRE BURSTS AND EVEN A FEW BLACK HOLES. THERE ARE ALWAYS A FEW BLACK HOLES IN EVERY GALAXY.

THE SQUIZZLESKWAKS ARE A MERRY LITTLE BAND OF EXTRATERRESTRIALS ALWAYS BY OLLY'S SIDE. NO COSMIC ADVENTURE IS TOO SMALL FOR THESE FUN-LOVING CREATURES THAT SUSTAIN THEIR CONSTANT DESIRE FOR NEW DISCOVERIES BY GOBBLING DOWN PLANET OOGLEBERRY CRYSTALS.

EVER WONDER WHY YOU'RE ON THIS TINY LITTLE PLANET IN THE MIDDLE OF A TINY LITTLE GALAXY AMIDST AN INFINITE UNIVERSE OF STARS, AND PLANETS? BE/SEE/DO SOMETHING GREAT WHILE YOU'RE HERE. YOU ONLY GET ONE CHANCE.

THE BIG BANG WAS A BLAST!
PICK ME! PICK ME!
I'VE GOT MAD SKILLS!
ME! ME! ME!
HE'S OFF HIS AXIS
I'M WITH THE ALIEN!
"OLLY, YOU ALONE WILL NOT BE ABLE TO SAVE EARTH. AS IN LIFE, YOU WILL NEED THE HELP OF OTHERS ALONG YOUR JOURNEY. LEAVE NO CRYSTAL UNTURNED AS YOU LOOK ACROSS ALL OF PLANET OOGLEBERRY TO SELECT YOUR CREW. ALWAYS LOOK FOR IMPORTANT QUALITIES IN OTHERS THAT MAY BE HELPFUL TO YOU IN YOUR QUEST."

NOT BOUND BY LAWS OF PHYSICS!
OVER HERE OLLY!
SPACED OUT
OVER HERE OLLY!
ADVENTURE IS MY ROCKET FUEL!
THROUGHOUT YOUR LIFE YOU'LL MEET LOTS OF CHARACTERS, BUT ALWAYS REMEMBER TO CHOOSE YOUR FRIENDS WISELY.

MEET THE SQUIZZLESKWAKS!

PAXION
THE PASSIONATE ONE

PAXION IS THE MOST PASSIONATE SQUIZZLESKWAK. REGARDLESS OF THE TASK, PAXION PUTS EVERY OUNCE OF ENERGY INTO EVERYTHING HE DOES, ELEVATES THOSE AROUND HIM AND ALWAYS ACHIEVES GREAT THINGS AS A RESULT.

DASHURI
LOVER OF ALL THINGS

DASHURI LOVES EVERYTHING ABOUT LIFE. FROM THE WAY OOGLEBERRY CRYSTALS GLISTEN IN THE MORNING LIGHT TO THE GLOW OF A FULL MOON AS IT SHINES DOWN ON EARTH AT MIDNIGHT, DASHURI LOVES EVERY MOMENT AND SO SHOULD YOU.

THE SQUIZZLESKWAKS GET THEIR NAME FROM THE SOUND THEY MAKE WHEN SEARCHING FOR OOGLEBERRY CRYSTALS.

USKO
THE FAITHFUL ONE
USKO IS THE MOST FAITHFUL FIDDLEFUNK. HAVING FAITH IS AN IMPORTANT CHARACTERISTIC FOR ADVENTURERS BECAUSE EVERY FIDDLEFUNK KNOWS NOT EVERYTHING GOES ACCORDING TO PLAN. USKO KNOWS THAT EVERYTHING WILL BE OK AS LONG AS YOU NEVER LOSE YOUR FAITH.

TIYAGA
THE PERSISTENT ONE
TIYAGA NEVER EVER GIVES UP. THAT'S WHY HE'S TAKEN THE EARTHLING NAME FOR PERSEVERANCE. BECAUSE WHEN YOU'RE AN ALIEN HURLING THROUGH DISTANT GALAXIES YOU'LL NEED TO STAY STRONG IN THE FACE OF ADVERSITY TO GET WHERE YOU WANT TO GO.

GUU
THE FRIENDLY ONE
GUU IS THE FRIENDLIEST FIDDLEFUNK. GUU HAS NEVER MET ANYONE HE DIDN'T LIKE AND HIS FELLOW FIDDLEFUNKS KNOW THEY CAN ALWAYS COUNT ON HIM THROUGH THICK AND THIN, A VERY IMPORTANT QUALITY IN BEING A TRUE FRIEND.

THE FIDDLEFUNKS ARE NOT SHY. IN FACT, THEY'LL COME UP AND SIT ON YOUR LAP IF GIVEN THE CHANCE.

INTRODUCING THE
FIDDLEFUNKS!

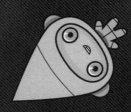

TIPUS
THE KIND ONE

TIPUS IS THE KINDEST FIDDLEFUNK. WHILE THE OTHER FIDDLEFUNKS LOOK FOR MISCHIEF, TIPUS SEEKS THE FRIENDSHIP OF STRANGERS AND IS ALWAYS PERFORMING RANDOM ACTS OF KINDNESS.

KWAAD
THE MISCHIEVOUS ONE

KWAAD IS THE MOST MISCHIEVOUS FIDDLEFUNK. EVERY ADVENTURER NEEDS SOME ADVENTURE, RIGHT? KWAAD IS THE MOST LIKELY ONE TO STIR UP TROUBLE AS THE FIDDLEFUNKS TRAVEL ACROSS DISTANT GALAXIES SEARCHING FOR ADVENTURE AND DISCOVERY.

LIFE IS ALL ABOUT THE JOURNEY OF FINDING YOUR GIFT. DON'T WASTE A MOMENT OF YOUR LIFE NOT PURSUING YOUR DREAMS.

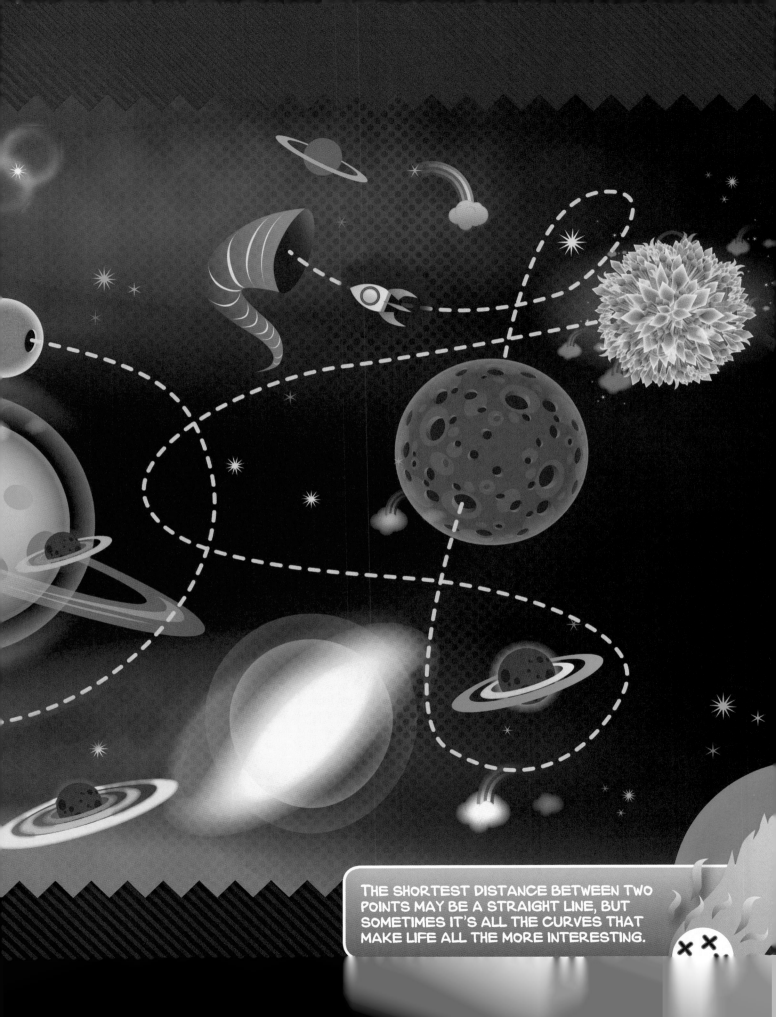

THE SHORTEST DISTANCE BETWEEN TWO POINTS MAY BE A STRAIGHT LINE, BUT SOMETIMES IT'S ALL THE CURVES THAT MAKE LIFE ALL THE MORE INTERESTING.

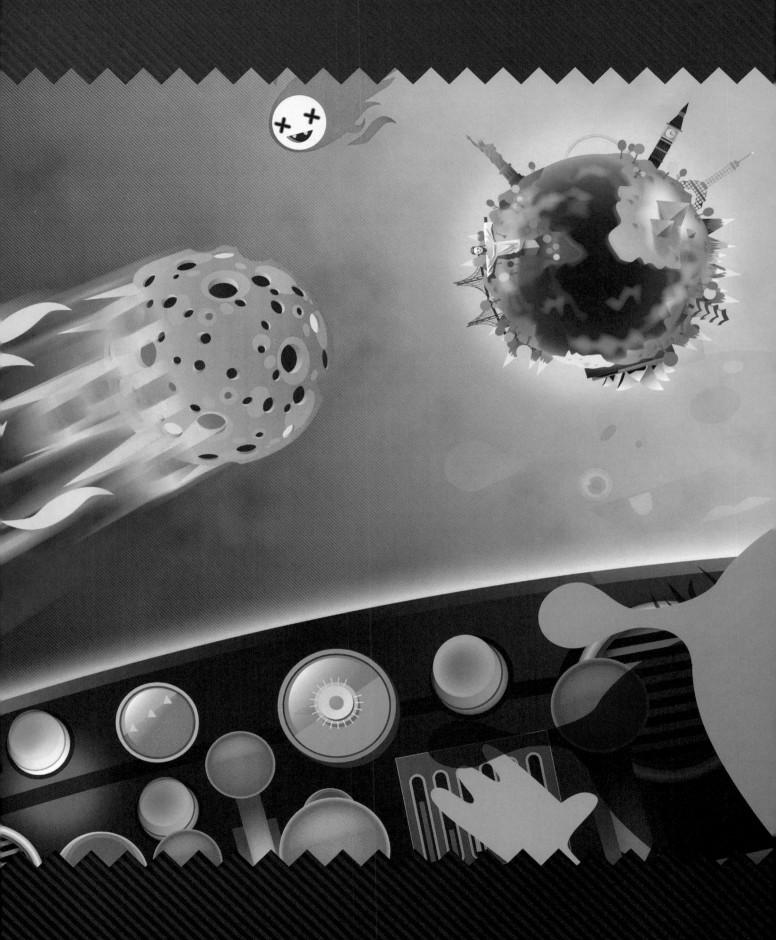

DURING YOUR LIFE, YOU'LL HAVE THE OPPORTUNITY TO SEE 28,470 SUNSETS, 390 ECLIPSES AND 936 FULL MOONS. MAKE THE MOST OF EVERY ONE.

THIS UFO IS
OUT OF GAS!

ALERT! 100

fuel cells low!

OUT OF LUCK

FUEL LOW!
WARNING!

HAVE FUN AND NEVER LOSE THAT
SPRING IN YOUR STEP (EVEN WITH
THE FORCE OF GRAVITY TRYING TO
PULL YOU DOWN).

KWAAD'S JOURNEY ENDS AMIDST A SEA OF PENGUINS WHO ARE NOT PARTICULARLY INTERESTED IN SHARING THE WORLD FAMOUS BOULDER BEACH WITH THEIR NEWFOUND FRIEND.
< CAPETOWN
MUMBAI >
< RIO DE JANEIRO
BOULDER BEACH
MADAGASCAR >
SOUTH AFRICA IS AN INCREDIBLY DIVERSE COUNTRY WITH MORE THAN 11 OFFICIAL LANGUAGES.

IT IS COMMON FOR FRENCH PEOPLE TO GREET EACH OTHER WITH A KISS OR TWO ON THE CHEEK. IT'S CALLED 'LA BISE.'

HANGING DELICATELY FROM THE VERY TOP OF THE EIFFEL TOWER, PAXION HAS A BIRD'S EYE VIEW OF PARIS, FRANCE, OTHERWISE KNOWN AS THE CITY OF LOVE AND LIGHT.

THE EARTH REVOLVES AT 1,038 MILES PER HOUR. ARE YOU FEELING DIZZY YET?

DON'T GIVE UP ON
YOUR DREAMS. EVER.

THE END

www.OllyOogleberry.com

www.Facebook.com/OllyOogleberry

COUNT YOUR LUCKY STARS EVERY DAY. NOW GET
OFF YOUR COUCH, PUT DOWN THE GADGETS AND
GO OUTSIDE TO DISCOVER ALL THE WONDERS OF
YOUR LOVELY LITTLE PLANET EARTH.

SHOP.OLLYOo

MOBILE CASES

APPAREL

PLUSH

BOOK

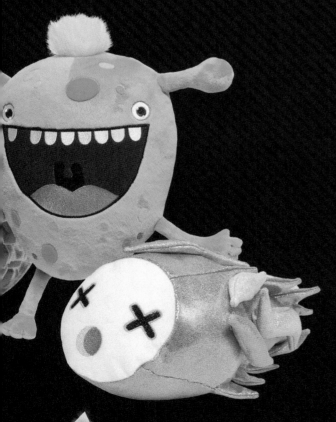

POSTER

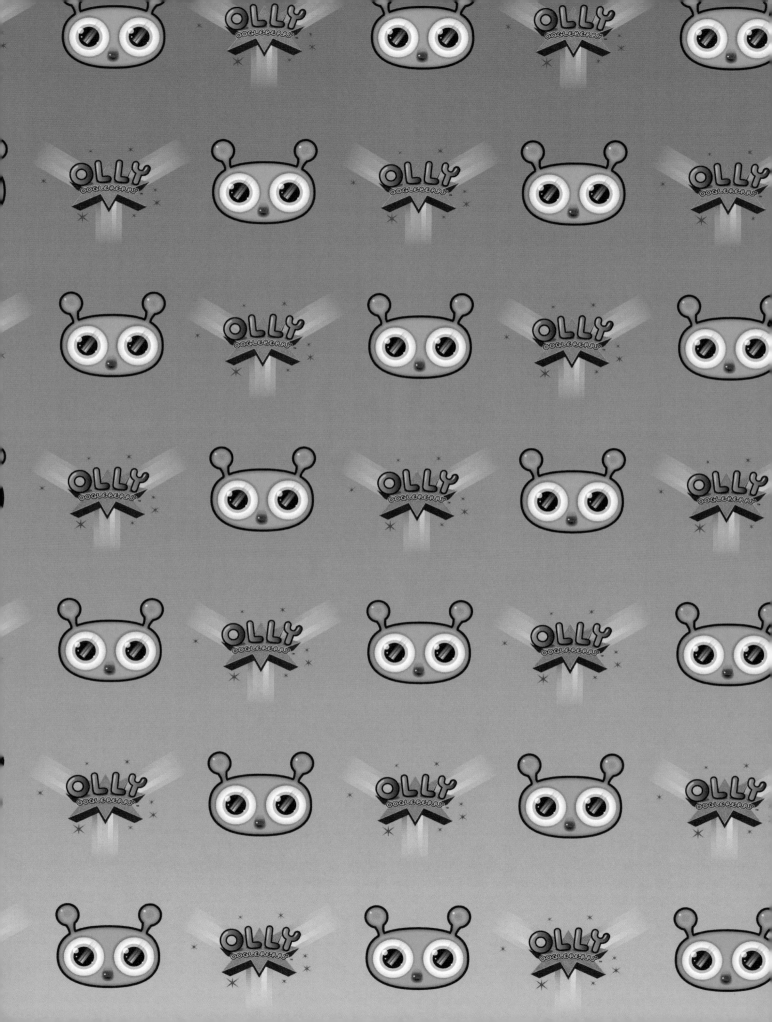

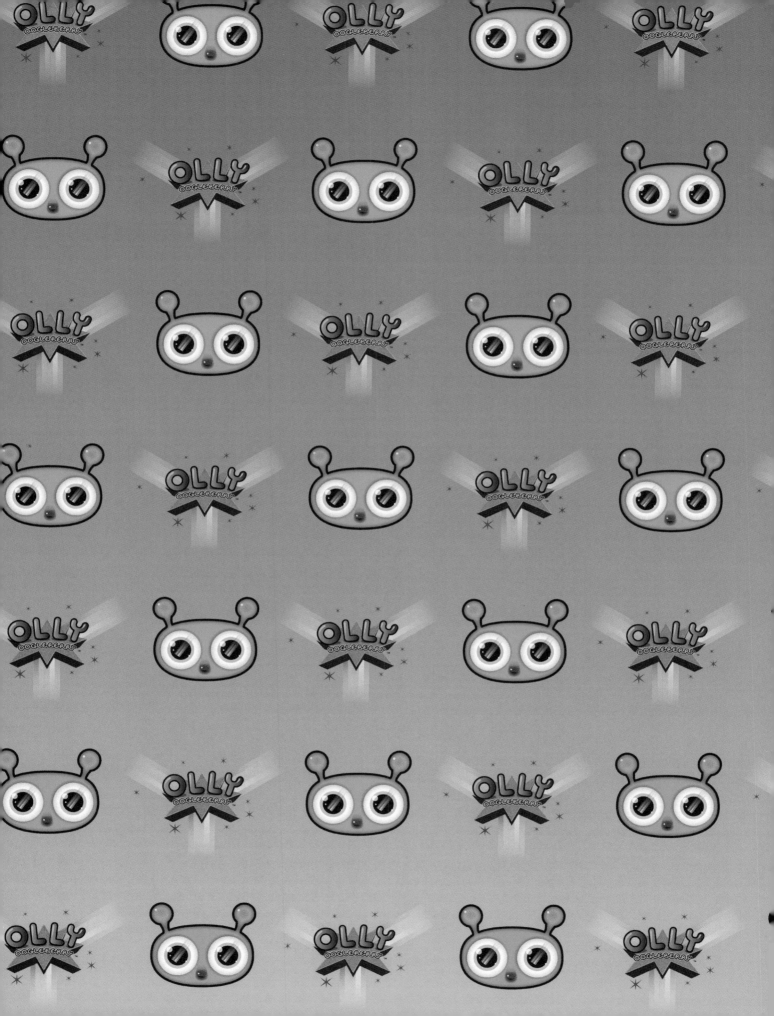

THE ALIEN HAS LANDED.

- ☑ MEET THE CHARACTERS
- ☑ OLLY SIGHTINGS
- ☑ EDUCATIONAL VIDEOS
- ☑ BACKSTORY
- ☑ GAMES & EXPERIMENTS
- ☑ OLLY'S ONLINE SHOP

WWW.OLLYOOGLEBERRY.COM

16389421R00028

Made in the USA
Charleston, SC
18 December 2012